BENNY'S
TRUE
COLORS

For Mike,
who from the beginning
believed in me and my dreams
–N.P.

To all the trans
and gender-nonconforming kids out there—
you got this
–A.P.

[Imprint]
MAKE YOUR MARK
NEW YORK

Written by Norene Paulson Illustrated by Anne Passchier

Benny looks like all the other little brown bats in the park—
he has a brown, furry body, webbed wings, and pointed ears.

But Benny isn't a bat.
Bats sleep upside down in dark places.
Benny likes warm sunshine better.

At night, bats fly around eating bugs.
Benny hates the taste of bugs, and they have
all those squirmy legs—YUCK!

Yes, on the outside, Benny *looks*
like a bat, but on the inside Benny
*knows* he is really . . .

. . . a BUTTERFLY.

Most nights, while Momma feasts on flying insects,
Benny dreams about a silky, soft body;
fluttering, patterned, colorful wings;
and long, curling antennae.

At bedtime, Momma always says,
"I love you, Benny."

Then she goes to sleep for the day
while Benny flies off to
the butterfly garden to practice
his butterfly moves.

But day after day,
his wings flap instead of flutter,

his ears twitch instead of curl,

and when he tries to land upright . . .
*Ouch!*

"Are you okay?"
asks Penelope the butterfly.

“Yes . . . I mean, no.” Benny can’t stop staring at her outstretched, beautifully patterned wings.

“Why?” Penelope asks.

"I am a butterfly like you—so I want colorful, patterned wings to flutter when I fly, like yours."

"I want my *outside* to match who I am *inside*!" he says.

Benny covers his face.
He waits for the butterflies to laugh at him.

But he doesn't hear anything.
He peeks out to see all the butterflies
fluttering their wings, waving their antennae,
encouraging him to follow them.

The rest of the day, and each day after that, they help him practice.
No matter what he does, they cheer for him.

One night, as other bats swoop through the air,
gobbling mosquitoes and beetles and moths,
Benny tells Momma that he has an idea.

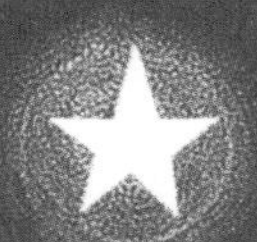

Momma hugs him and says,
"I am here for you."

The next day, Benny asks his friends, "Will you help me?"

Penelope and the other butterflies listen closely while Benny tells them his plan.

"You are already one of us," says Penelope.
"You don't have to change anything."

"I know," says Benny.
"I'm doing this for me."

The next morning, Penelope is waiting in the garden with three caterpillars. They measure Benny from the tip of his nose to the tips of his wings.

"Well?" asks Penelope.

"Our silk is the strongest," says one caterpillar.

"The best of the best," agrees another.
"I think it will work!" cries the third.
"Ready?" Penelope asks Benny.

“Ready,” Benny says.

Then he hangs upside down while the caterpillars, using their special silk, weave a snug cocoon around his body.

Before falling asleep,
Benny hears Momma
say, “I love you.”

Inside the silk, under watchful eyes,
Benny slowly changes.

His webbed wings split into colorful, patterned scales. His ears lengthen and narrow into antennae.

And when all the changes are done, Benny wriggles free.

Everyone cheers
as Benny flutters his new wings,
gently unfurls his antennae,
and takes a short, graceful hop into the air.

When he sees Momma, Benny squeaks loudly,
"I love you, Momma!"

"Oh, Benny!
I *always* have and *always* will
love YOU!" she says.

[Imprint]
MAKE YOUR MARK
A part of Macmillan Publishing Group, LLC
120 Broadway, New York, NY 10271

ABOUT THIS BOOK
The art in this book was created digitally. The text was set in ITC Stone Informal, and the display type is Montecatini Pro. The book was edited by Erin Stein and designed by Natalie C. Sousa. The production was supervised by Raymond Ernesto Colon, and the production editor was Dawn Ryan.


Printed in China by RR Donnelley Asia Printing Solutions Ltd., Dongguan City, Guangdong Province.

Library of Congress Cataloging-in-Publication Data

Names: Paulson, Norene, author. | Passchier, Anne, illustrator.
Title: Benny's true colors / written by Norene Paulson ; illustrated by Anne Passchier.
Description: First edition. | New York : Imprint, 2020. | Audience: Ages 3-7. | Audience: Grades K-1. |
Summary: Although Benny looks like a bat, he knows he is a butterfly and, with the support of his mother and friends, finds a way to make his outside match who he is inside.
Identifiers: LCCN 2020009801 | ISBN 9781250207715 (hardcover)
Subjects: CYAC: Identity—Fiction. | Bats—Fiction. | Butterflies—Fiction.
Classification: LCC PZ7.1.P38535 Ben 2020 | DDC [E]—dc23
LC record available at https://lccn.loc.gov/2020009801

ISBN 978-1-250-20771-5 (hardcover)



Imprint logo designed by Amanda Spielman

First edition, 2020

1 3 5 7 9 10 8 6 4 2

mackids.com

Anyone who doth dare
Steal this book, alas, beware!
A colony of bats,
A swarm of butterflies
Will follow thee far,
Will follow thee wide
Fluttering and flapping their wings to chastise!
From them, thou cannot hide.
Perchance, 'tis best thee put this book aside.